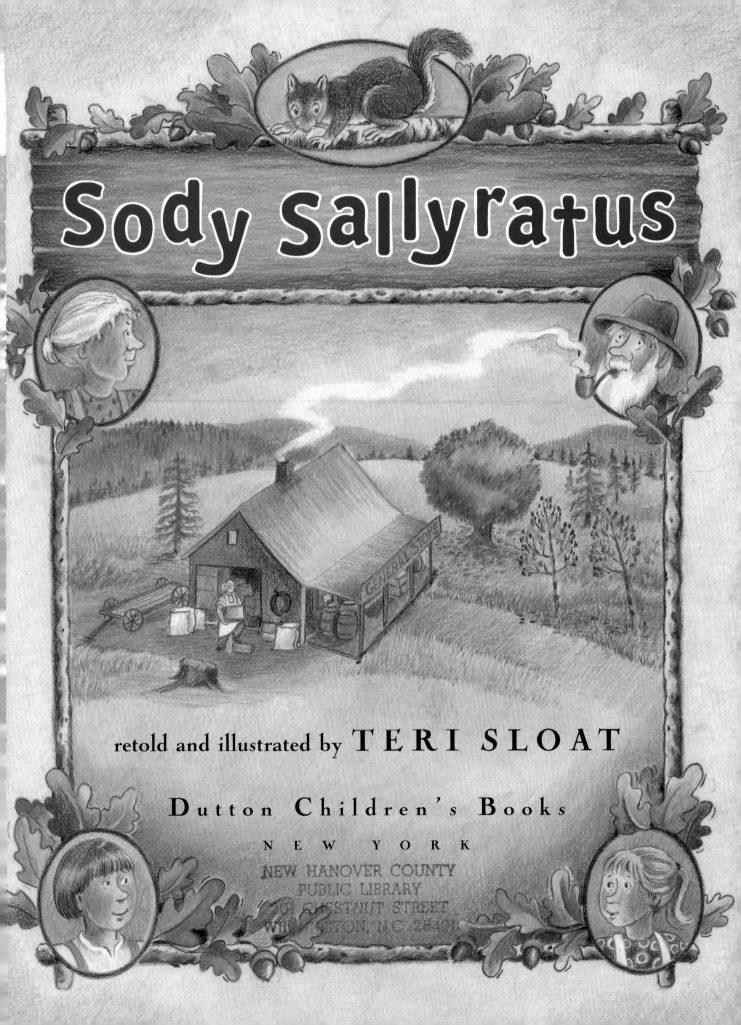

Sody Sallyratus

retold and illustrated by TERI SLOAT

Dutton Children's Books

NEW YORK

Author's Note

This story from the Appalachian Mountains has been retold
in several versions, which are based most probably on
Richard Chase's retelling in *Grandfather Tales* (1948).
Sody Sallyratus has a basic form that allows the author to
create a rhythm and repetition as it is told. A favorite with
storytellers, it is included in Margaret MacDonald's
Twenty Tellable Tales, among other collections.
With due respect for the intelligence and lifestyle of the big
black bear, in my version I have given him a home in
the berry patch, and have let him escape to a new
life after giving up overeating.

Library of Congress Cataloging-in-Publication Data

Sloat, Teri.
Sody sallyratus/by Teri Sloat [author/illustrator].
—1st ed.   p. cm.
Summary: When one after another family member goes to the
store for baking soda and never returns, the pet squirrel
decides to investigate.
ISBN 0-525-45609-0
[1. Squirrels—Fiction. 2. Bears—Fiction. 3. Humorous stories.]
I. Title. PZ7.S633154So 1997
[E]—dc20 96-14686 CIP AC

Published in the United States 1997 by Dutton Children's Books,
a division of Penguin Books USA Inc.
375 Hudson Street, New York, New York 10014
Designed by Sara Reynolds
Printed in Hong Kong
First Edition
1 3 5 7 9 10 8 6 4 2

To Steve and Nelda, voices we love

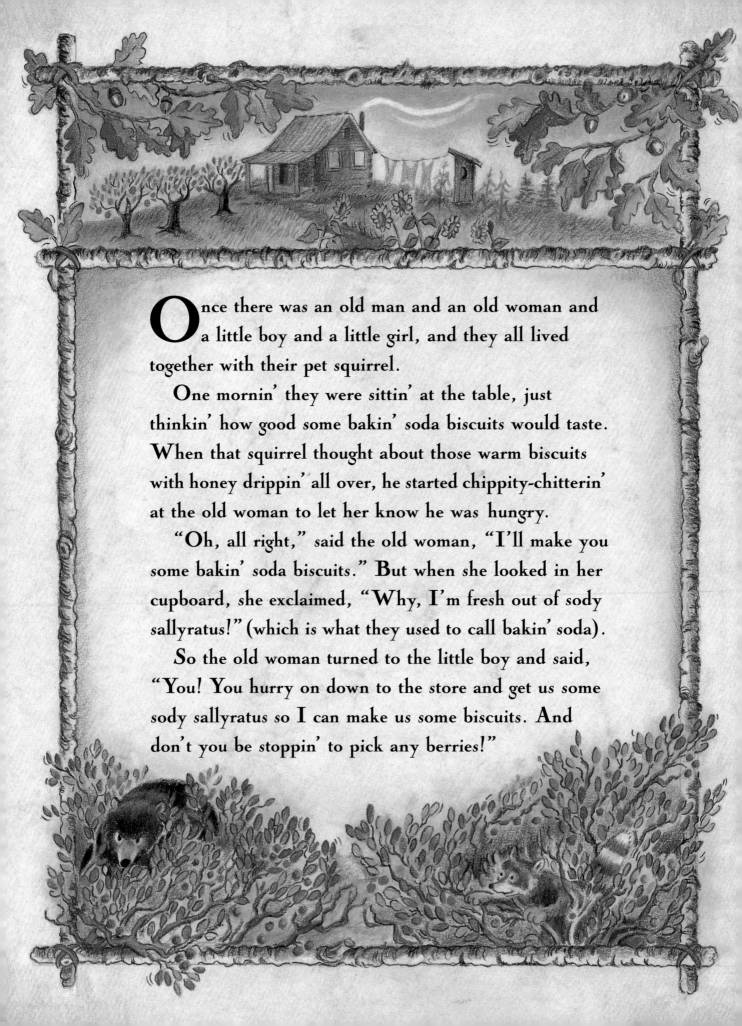

Once there was an old man and an old woman and a little boy and a little girl, and they all lived together with their pet squirrel.

One mornin' they were sittin' at the table, just thinkin' how good some bakin' soda biscuits would taste. When that squirrel thought about those warm biscuits with honey drippin' all over, he started chippity-chitterin' at the old woman to let her know he was hungry.

"Oh, all right," said the old woman, "I'll make you some bakin' soda biscuits." But when she looked in her cupboard, she exclaimed, "Why, I'm fresh out of sody sallyratus!" (which is what they used to call bakin' soda).

So the old woman turned to the little boy and said, "You! You hurry on down to the store and get us some sody sallyratus so I can make us some biscuits. And don't you be stoppin' to pick any berries!"

That little boy went skippin' out the door, and just so he wouldn't be forgettin' what he was goin' after, he played a tune on his harmonica that went up and down like the mountains. He was playin' SODY SODY SODY SALLYRATUS.

He skipped on down the road, through the berry
patch, and into the store.

The storekeeper filled his little bag with bakin' soda.

"Thank ya kindly," said the little boy, and he went
skippin' back down the road. When he came to the
berry patch, he stopped, and he was pickin' himself
some berries when...

UP JUMPED A BIG BLACK BEAR!
That big black bear looked down at that little boy pickin' his berries and said, "I'm gonna eat you up!" And he did.

Back at the cabin, the old man and the old woman and the little girl were still sittin' at the table, waitin' for that little boy to come back. Pretty soon, that squirrel started his chippity-chitterin' again.

When that old woman heard that hungry squirrel, she looked at the little girl and said, "You! You go on down to the store and see what's keepin' that little boy! And don't you be stoppin' to pick any berries!"

So that little girl went dancin' on out the door, and just so she wouldn't be forgettin' what she was goin' after, she whistled a tune that went up and down like the mountains. She was whistlin' SODY SODY SODY SALLYRATUS.

She danced on down the road, through the berry patch, and into the store. She asked the storekeeper if he'd seen that little boy.

"Why, he's done been here and gone, and I gave him his sody sallyratus. I'll bet you he's down in the berry patch, pickin' berries."

"Thank ya kindly," said the little girl, and she went dancin' out the door and back down the road. But when she came to the berry patch, she stopped to look for the little boy. And while she was lookin', she was pickin' berries, and pretty soon...

UP JUMPED A BIG BLACK BEAR!

That big black bear looked down at that little girl pickin' his berries, and he said, "I just ate me a little boy and his sody sallyratus, and I'm gonna eat you, too!"

And he did!

Now, back at the cabin, that old man and that old woman were still sittin' and waitin' and thinkin' 'bout those biscuits, and they'd still be sittin' there if that squirrel hadn't started his chippity-chitterin' again.

When the old woman heard that hungry squirrel, she looked at the old man and said, "You! You go on down to the store and see what's keepin' those young'uns of ours. And don't you be stoppin' to pick any berries!"

So that old man went shufflin' on out the door, and just so he wouldn't be forgettin' what he was goin' after, he was puffin' on his pipe and blowin' smoke rings that went up and down like the mountains. They spelled **SODY SODY SODY SALLYRATUS**.

He shuffled right on down the road, through the berry patch, and when he got to the store, he asked the storekeeper if he'd seen those young'uns of his.

"Why, they've both done been here and gone, and I gave that boy his sody sallyratus. I'll bet you they're down in the berry patch, pickin' berries."

"Thank ya kindly," said the old man, and he went shufflin' down the road. When he came to the berry patch, he stopped to look for those young'uns, and while he was lookin', he was pickin' berries, and pretty soon...

UP JUMPED A BIG BLACK BEAR!

That big black bear looked down at that old man pickin' his berries, and he said, "I just ate me a little boy and his sody sallyratus, and I ate me a sweet little girl, and I'm gonna eat you, too!"

And he did!

Back at the cabin, the old woman was still sittin' and waitin' to make those biscuits when that squirrel started his chippity-chitterin' again.

The old woman looked at that hungry squirrel and said, "Sometimes the only way to get something done is to go and do it yourself!"

So that old woman—she went stompin' down the road with a bee in her bonnet that flew out and started buzzin' up and down like the mountains. It was buzzin' the words SODY SODY SODY SALLYRATUS.

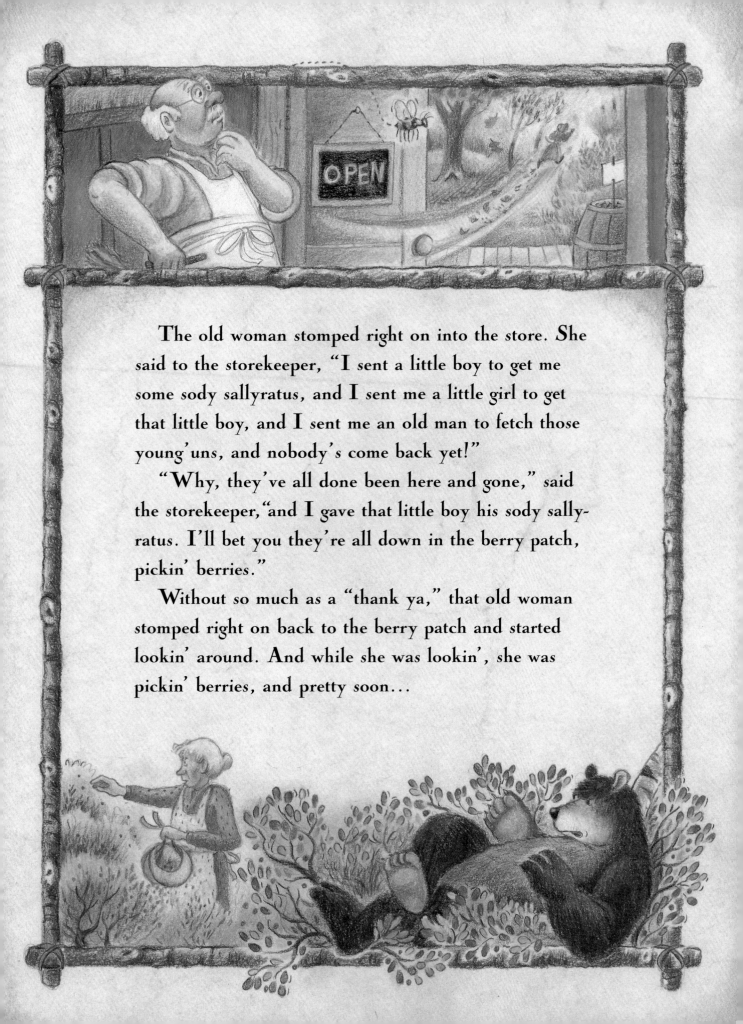

The old woman stomped right on into the store. She said to the storekeeper, "I sent a little boy to get me some sody sallyratus, and I sent me a little girl to get that little boy, and I sent me an old man to fetch those young'uns, and nobody's come back yet!"

"Why, they've all done been here and gone," said the storekeeper, "and I gave that little boy his sody sallyratus. I'll bet you they're all down in the berry patch, pickin' berries."

Without so much as a "thank ya," that old woman stomped right on back to the berry patch and started lookin' around. And while she was lookin', she was pickin' berries, and pretty soon...

UP JUMPED A BIG BLACK BEAR!

That big black bear looked down at that old woman pickin' his berries, and he said, "I just ate me a little boy and his sody sallyratus, and I ate me a sweet little girl, and I ate me the toughest old man, and I'm gonna eat you, too!"

And he did!

Back at the cabin, that pet squirrel was pacin' back and forth, and he couldn't wait much longer for those biscuits. So he said, "I'd better go see what's takin' everybody so long."

That squirrel hop-scatted down the road, through the berry patch, and into the store, and he jumped right up onto the counter. With his chippity-chitterin' squirrel talk, he asked the storekeeper why nobody'd come back to make him his bakin' soda biscuits.

The storekeeper said, "They've all done been here and gone, and I just know they're all down in the berry patch, pickin' berries."

That squirrel hop-scatted as fast as he could, back to the berry patch, and started lookin' for everybody. But while he was lookin', he was pickin' berries, and pretty soon, **UP JUMPED A BIG BLACK BEAR!**

When that big black bear looked down at that little chippity-chitterin' squirrel, he just laughed and said, "I just ate me a little boy and his sody sallyratus, and I ate me the sweetest little girl, and the toughest old man, and the stringiest old woman. I've got room for one more bite, so I'm gonna eat you, too!"

But before he knew it, that squirrel had hop-scatted right on up a tree.

The bear looked up at that squirrel and said, "If you can make it up that tree with those little feet of yours, I know I can make it with these big feet of mine." And the bear went scramblin' up the tree after that squirrel.

When the squirrel was almost to the top of that tree, he hop-scatted out on a limb. So the bear went out on the limb after him. That tree was swayin' back and forth, and back and forth, so that squirrel took a jump and landed in the top of another tree.

The bear looked over at that squirrel and said, "If you can jump that far with those little feet of yours, I know I can jump that far with these big feet of mine."

The next time that tree swayed back and forth, that bear took off, but...

...he didn't quite make it.

He hit the ground so hard that they all flew out—the little boy and his sody sallyratus, and the little girl, and the old man, and the old woman.

They all followed the squirrel back to the cabin, and that old woman baked the biggest batch of bakin' soda biscuits you've ever seen.

There was one for the old woman, one for the old man, one for the little boy, and one for the little girl.

The rest were for that pet squirrel so he'd stop makin' those chippity-chitterin' hungry sounds.

The Old Woman's Bakin' Soda Biscuits

2 cups flour

3/4 teaspoon sody sallyratus
   (baking soda)

1 1/2 teaspoons cream of tartar

1/2 teaspoon salt

1/2 cup butter

1/2 cup milk

2 eggs

- Put enough wood in the firebox to heat the oven to 400 degrees. Then put the flour, sody sallyratus, cream of tartar, and salt in a bowl; sift them together with your fingers.
- Work the butter into that dry stuff till the mixture looks like little crumbs.
- Stir in milk and eggs. Keep stirrin' till the dough follows the fork 'round the bowl.
- Knead the dough about twenty times on a well-floured surface.
- Cut out a dozen big biscuits and bake 12-15 minutes.
- Eat those biscuits while they're still warm, and don't you be forgettin' the butter and honey on top.

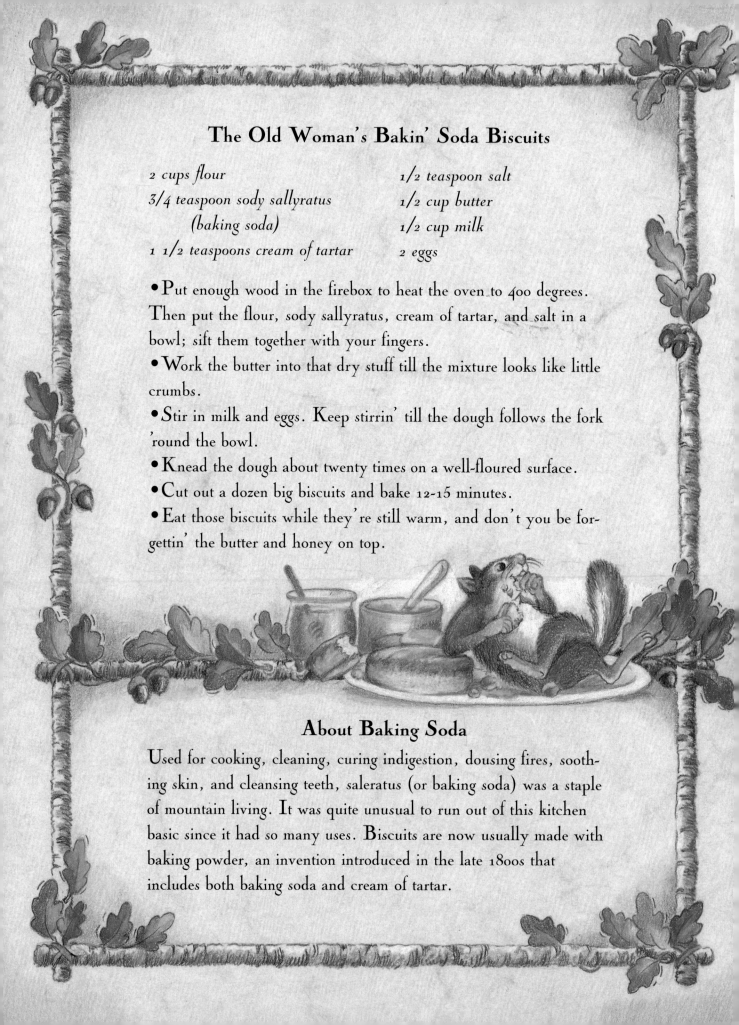

About Baking Soda

Used for cooking, cleaning, curing indigestion, dousing fires, soothing skin, and cleansing teeth, saleratus (or baking soda) was a staple of mountain living. It was quite unusual to run out of this kitchen basic since it had so many uses. Biscuits are now usually made with baking powder, an invention introduced in the late 1800s that includes both baking soda and cream of tartar.